For Ramona, I know you'll make giant footprints on this earth.
—MG

For Catharine Kim Wooden, my forever yogi.
—MR

Sounds True | Boulder, CO 80306

Text © 2019 by Mariam Gates | Illustrations © 2019 by Matthew Rivera

Published 2019

Cover and book design by Karen Polaski | Printed in South Korea

Library of Congress Cataloging-in-Publication Data

Names: Gates, Mariam, author. | Rivera, Matthew (Children's books illustrator), illustrator.

Title: Dinosaur yoga / by Mariam Gates ; illustrated by Matthew Rivera.

Description: Boulder, Colorado : Sounds True, 2019. | Summary: Illustrations and simple, rhyming text portray a
variety of dinosaurs as they lift spiky frills, bend bumpy knees, and breathe through snouts while trying yoga poses.

Identifiers: LCCN 2018057383 (print) | LCCN 2018059927 (ebook)
ISBN 9781683643050 (ebook) | ISBN 9781683643043 (hardcover)

Subjects: | CYAC: Stories in rhyme. | Yoga--Fiction. | Dinosaurs--Fiction.

Classification: LCC PZ8.3.G2114 (ebook) | LCC PZ8.3.G2114 Din 2019 (print) | DDC [E]--dc23

LC record available at https://lccn.loc.gov/2018057383

10 9 8 7 6 5 4 3 2 1

Dinosaur Yoga

written by
Mariam Gates

illustrated by
Matthew Rivera

sounds true
BOULDER, COLORADO

Shhh—listen! There are dinosaurs nearby!

Do you hear them
crashing, bashing, thrashing
through the leafy green?

They have big teeth
and even bigger feet,
but they aren't trying to look mean.

Sometimes they are
sad or mad or tired
of waiting for a turn.

But these dinosaurs don't
want to knock down trees—
they are here to learn.

Today when they don't get their way,
they won't stomp on each other's toes.
Instead, these dinos will take a break
and try a yoga pose.

It's time for Dinosaur Yoga!

Start with a deep breath in
and a long breath out,

as you roar and reach to each side.

Then bend one knee
and focus

while you spread your
wings out wide.

Breathe in through your snout.
Breathe out.

With strong and steady legs, bend both knees now.
Press palm to palm,
claws pointed to the sky.

off the ground to balance,

Bring one mighty hind foot

lifting your spiky frills high.

Now straighten each scaly arm,
and fold slowly down, down, down.
Bend your bumpy knees a little
and almost touch the ground.

Calm and still,
breathe in through your snout.
Breathe out.

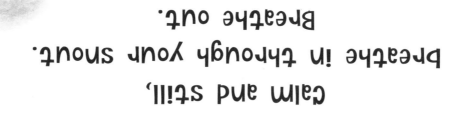

Let your shoulders, neck, and horned head
get heavy and hang low.
Sway your big body to feel where you're tight
and gently let it go.

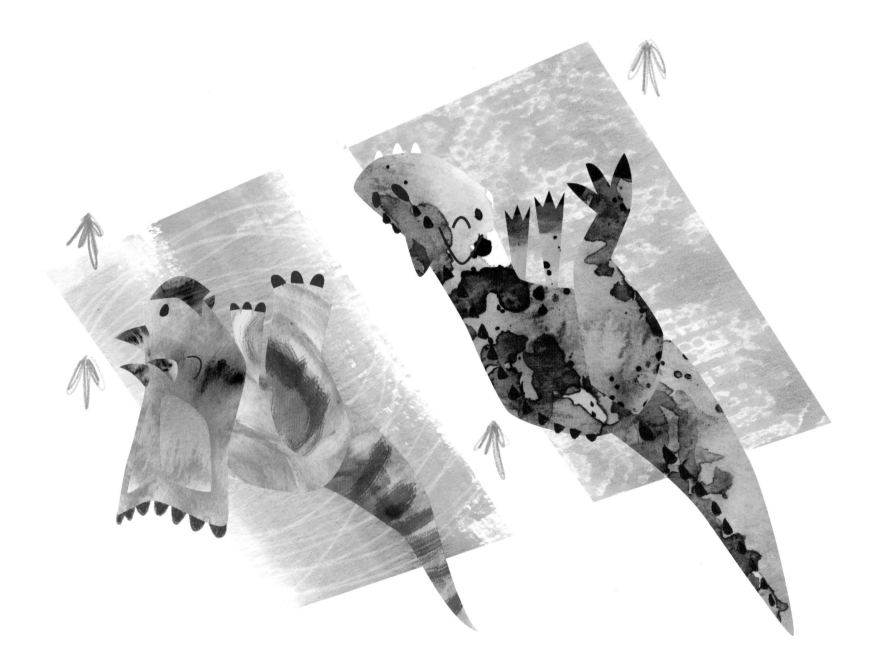

Breathe in through your snout. Breathe out.

Now stretch one enormous leg back like a tail,
as you lunge forward with a knobby knee.
Take a deep breath in and a looooong breath out,
and feel how calm and awake you can be.

With one knee down and
a taloned hand on the ground,
reach the other hand high
to make a straight line.

Open up as wide as you can and let your big heart shine.

Breathe in through your snout.
Breathe out.

Sit up and feel your
spiny spine grow tall.
Straighten one long leg
and cross the other over.
Twist and then release.

These dinosaurs are feeling better.
It's the most relaxed they've ever been.

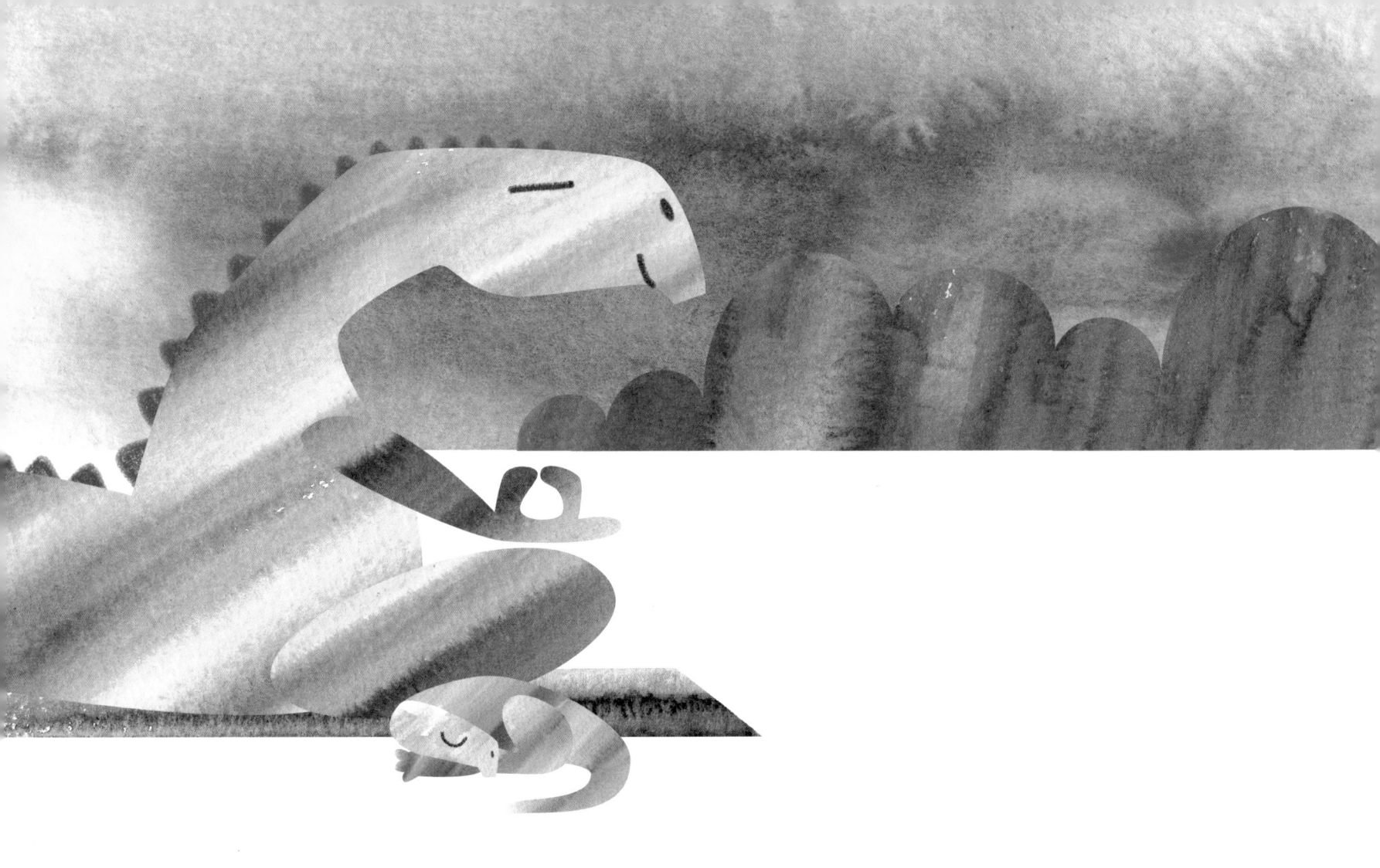

Their spines are long, their shoulders loose,
and they each have a toothy grin.

Sometimes they'll still get frustrated
and tight in their scaly skin.

But now when they need to calm themselves down,
they'll know exactly where to begin.

With Dinosaur Yoga!

Dinosaur Yoga

1 REVERSE WARRIOR

- Press both feet evenly into the ground.
- Reach your top hand high to the sky and place your bottom hand on your back thigh.
- Switch sides.

2 WARRIOR II

- Bend your front knee and keep it in line with your ankle.
- Keep both feet flat.
- Keep back leg straight.
- Reach your arms out wide.
- Switch sides.

6 LUNGE

- Stretch your back leg behind you.
- Bend your front knee and press your foot into the ground.
- Keep your knee in line with your ankle.
- Switch sides.

1 SIDE PLANK | ONE KNEE DOWN

- Place one knee on the ground and lean onto one hand.
- Reach your other arm straight up toward the sky.
- Switch sides.

Flow

③ HORSE

- Press your palms together in front of your chest.
- Roll your shoulders back.
- Bend your knees just a little out to the sides.

④ TREE

- Lengthen your spine.
- Rest your right foot on your left ankle or above your knee and balance.
- Switch sides.

⑤ FORWARD FOLD

- Bend your knees and fold over at the waist.
- Let your head and neck be very relaxed and hang down.

⑧ SEATED TWIST

- Sit up tall and straighten your right leg; cross your left leg over.
- Bring your elbow to your knee and twist all the way to one side.
- Switch sides.

⑨ CALM AND STILL

- Sit comfortably.
- Let your spine be long and roll your shoulders back.
- Rest your hands gently on your knees.

Dinosaur Fun Facts

PTERODACTYL

The Pterodactyl was actually a pterosaur, a type of flying reptile.

STEGOSAURUS

This herbivore's best defense was its powerful spiked tail.

ALLOSAURUS

This fierce dinosaur could shed its teeth and grow new ones.

TYRANNOSAURUS REX

This fierce carnivore's teeth were 12–13 inches long—the size of bananas!

CHASMOSAURUS

This dinosaur had a colorful frill on top of its head and a beak like a bird.

MAIASAURA

This dinosaur lived in enormous herds, and laid up to 40 eggs at a time.

UTAHRAPTOR

This carnivore walked on two feet and had a large 9-inch curved claw on each foot. It was named for the state where its fossils were discovered.

COMPSOGNATHUS

This carnivore was the size of a chicken, but it could run very fast, probably up to 40 miles an hour.

SPINOSAURUS

This dinosaur was the biggest carnivore on earth—bigger than the well-known T-Rex. It was about 50 feet in length and weighed as much as three elephants!

BRACHIOSAURUS

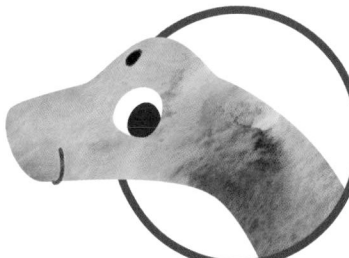

This herbivore with its long neck fed on the highest trees like a giraffe. It could eat leaves from branches 30 feet off the ground.

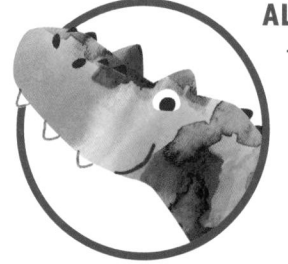

For Naoki & Pok

This edition first published in 2014 by Gecko Press
PO Box 9335, Marion Square, Wellington 6141, New Zealand
info@geckopress.com

English language edition © Gecko Press Ltd 2014
Translation © Bill Nagelkerke 2014

Copyright text and illustrations © 2005 by Sieb Posthuma, Amsterdam, Em. Querido's Uitgeverij B.V.
Original title: Waar is Rintje?

First American edition published in 2015 by Gecko Press USA, an imprint of Gecko Press Ltd.

Distributed in the United States and Canada by Lerner Publishing Group, www.lernerbooks.com
Distributed in the United Kingdom by Bounce Sales and Marketing, www.bouncemarketing.co.uk
Distributed in Australia by Scholastic Australia, www.scholastic.com.au
Distributed in New Zealand by Random House NZ, www.randomhouse.co.nz

A catalogue record for this book is available from the National Library of New Zealand.

Edited by Penelope Todd
Typeset by Vida & Luke Kelly, New Zealand
Printed in China by Everbest Printing Co Ltd, an accredited ISO 14001 & FSC certified printer

ISBN hardback: 978-1-927271-45-2
ISBN paperback: 978-1-927271-46-9
E-book available

This book was published with the support of the Dutch Foundation for Literature.

For more curiously good books, visit www.geckopress.com